# Grandma's Quilt

By Christy L. Viviano

Illustrated by Julie A. Martin

*To Mary and Kate
Sweet Dreams!*

*Julie A. Martin*

*Happy reading!*

*Christy L. Viviano*

TREE HOUSE PRESS, INC.

New Orleans

Request for permission to make copies of any part of the work should be mailed to:
Permissions Department, Tree House Press, Inc.
P.O. Box 7185, Opelousas, Louisiana 70571.

Library of Congress Number 96-061093

ISBN 1-881490-03-3

The original illustrations are drawings done in colored pencil.

Printed by Tien Wah Press,
Singapore

*To my mother
who covered all of us with her quilts,
and with her love.*

Christy Lawrence Viviano

*To Mama*

Julie Annette Martin

Katie Beth was staying at Grandma's for a whole week. By herself. For the first time.

Grandma brought Katie Beth upstairs to her bedroom. It was next to Grandma and Grandpa.

The bed was a tall four-poster, very high off the floor. Katie Beth usually slept in it with her sister, Lauren.

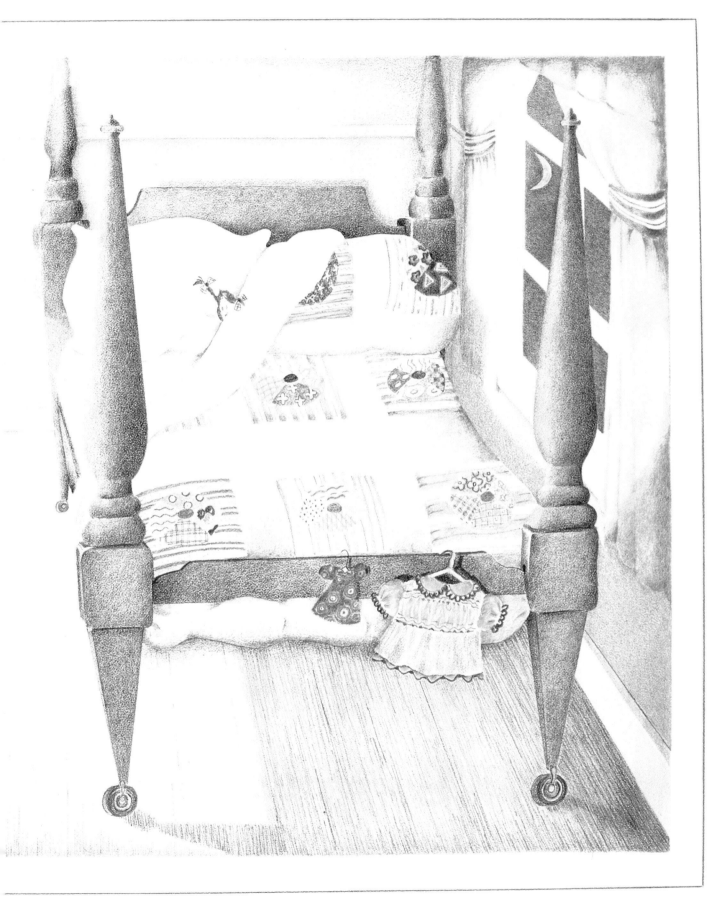

Tonight the bed seemed very empty,
and very far away from the floor.

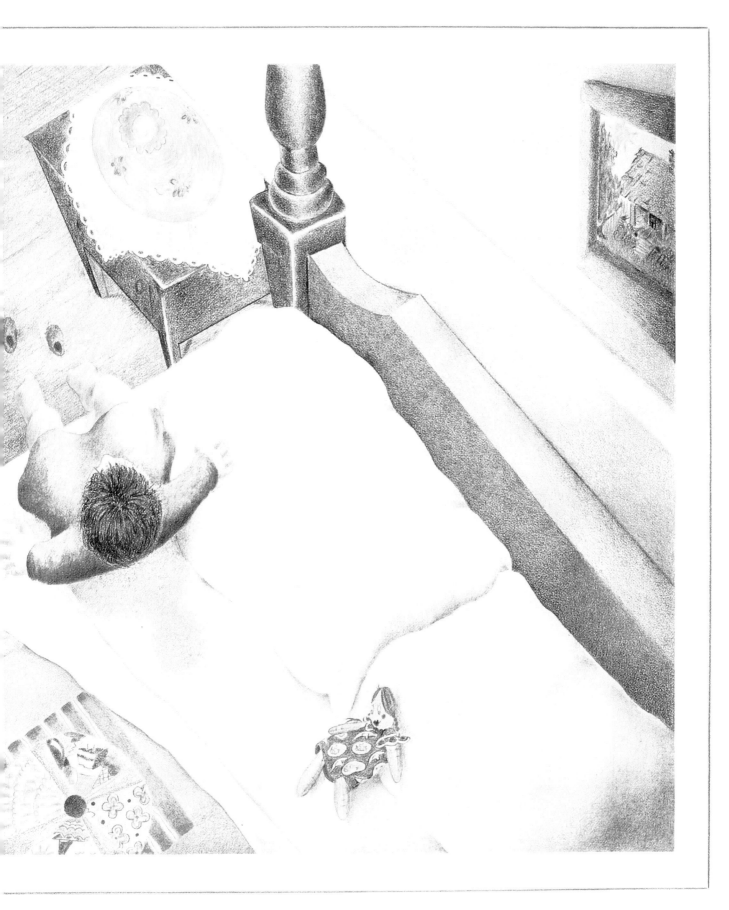

Grandma came to tuck her in and to kiss her good-night.

"Grandma," Katie Beth said in a small voice. "I'm sort of scared."

"Why, honey? We're next door."

"I know, but I'm all alone in here."

Grandma stroked Katie Beth's curls with a gentle hand. She pulled up the patchwork quilt and tucked it under the little girl's chin.

"Well, honey, that's where you're wrong. "

"What do you mean, Grandma?"

"Let me tell you a story or two, and you'll see what I mean."

"Now, do you see this little square right here? The one that is pink with tiny rosebuds?"

She pointed to a patch of color close to Katie Beth's chin.

"Do you know where this piece came from?"

"No," Katie Beth said.

"That's a part of the dress that you wore to your second birthday party. Do you remember it?"

Katie Beth's fingers touched the patch of soft pink cloth.

"Oh, yes," she said. "I remember that dress. I was sad when I outgrew it. It was my favorite dress when I was a little girl."

"Oh, look here, Katie Beth. I'll bet you remember this one."

Grandma showed her a patch of yellow with polka dots. Katie Beth frowned, trying to remember. Then she bounced up and down a little in the bed.

"I do! It's Lauren's Easter dress." She giggled. "Mama was so mad when she got paint all over it at the Easter egg hunt."

"Yes, she was. Your mama had smocked that dress by hand. You were supposed to have it when Lauren got too big for it."

"That's all right, Grandma. I like to have my own dresses," Katie Beth said.

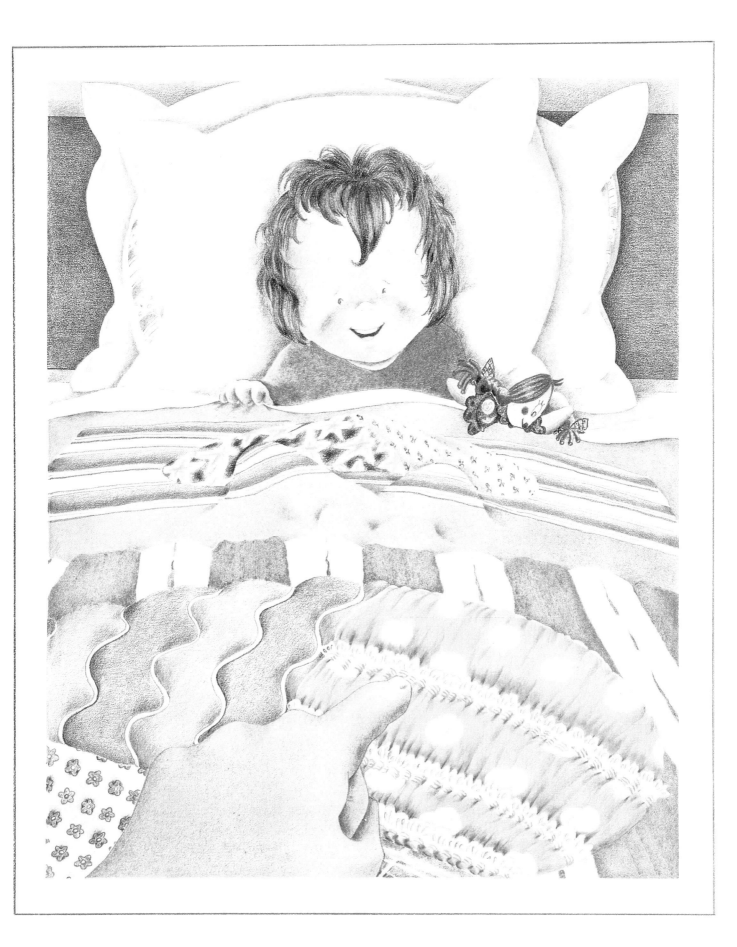

Grandma smiled and her finger travelled farther down the quilt and came to rest on a green plaid scrap.

"This one, now. This piece came from a shirt that your daddy wore when he was a little boy. He would come back from baseball practice with that shirt so muddy! It was his lucky game shirt," Grandma added.

"And look over here. This scrap with the bright yellow and red flowers. It came from your mother's dress, one that she wore in Hawaii when she and your daddy went there on their honeymoon."

"She was such a beautiful bride," Grandma went on. "I wish you could have seen her."

Katie Beth smiled and snuggled down under the quilt. She yawned a little.

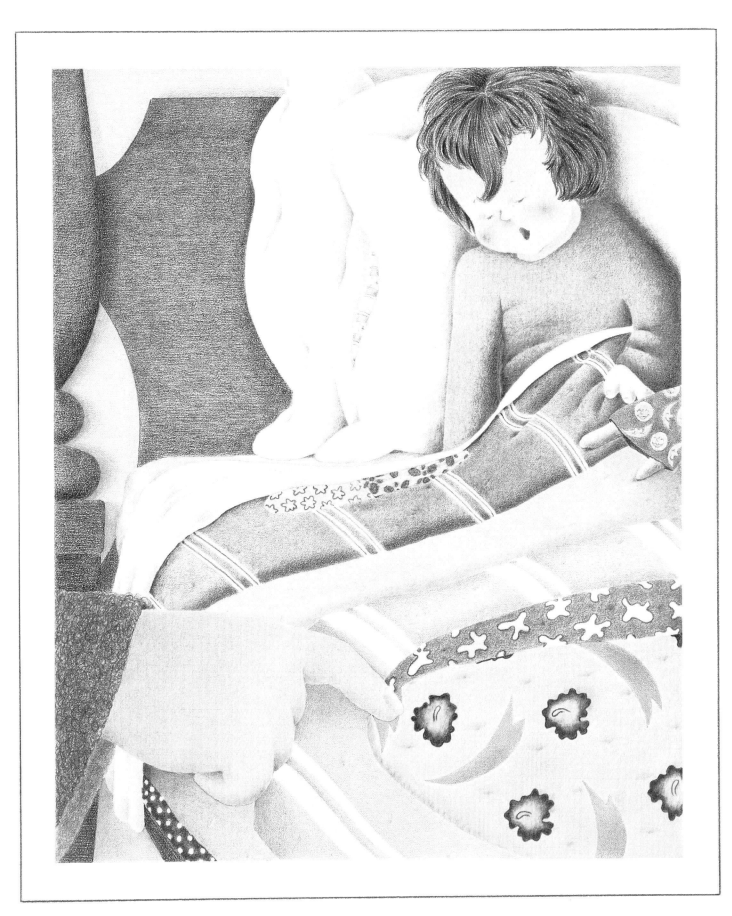

Grandma's voice changed then. She touched a patch in the middle of the quilt.

"This was from my favorite dress, a beautiful lavender color with white stripes. It had a full skirt and a white lace collar. I wore it when I was a young girl, before I met your Grandpa. It was the prettiest dress I ever had." She had a far away, remembering look on her face.

"It wasn't easy to get one from Grandpa," she went on. "He hated to let go of his clothes, especially ones he was comfortable with. But I finally persuaded him to let me have an old blue work shirt. Here it is."

Grandma's fingers touched a worn-looking scrap of light blue, so faded that it almost looked white.

"I sent him off to work on many mornings wearing that shirt," she said with a smile.

Katie Beth had to fight to keep her eyes open now.

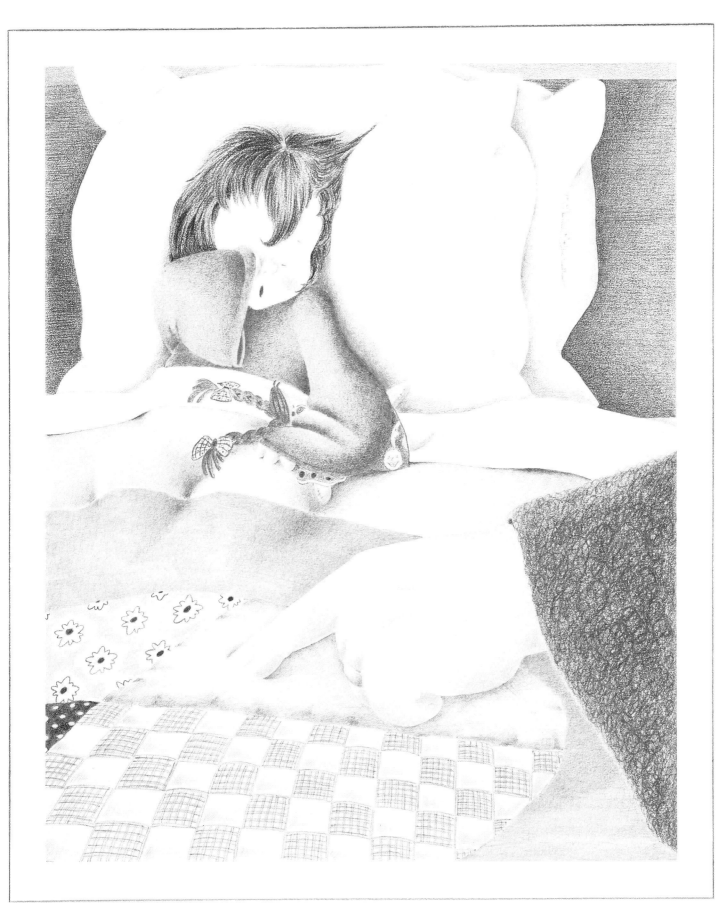

Grandma tucked the quilt up around her snugly. "I enjoyed making this quilt, Katie Beth," she explained.

"You see, I took the scraps from the clothes we all wore when we were happy, the ones that made us feel good when we wore them. They were really scraps of our lives."

She touched the little girl's cheek.

Then, softly, "So, you see, my darling Katie Beth, you are not alone in this bed. You have all these people with you while you sleep, watching over you. Making sure you have good dreams. You are not only covered with a quilt; you are covered with their love."

Katie Beth smiled, gave one more big yawn, and...

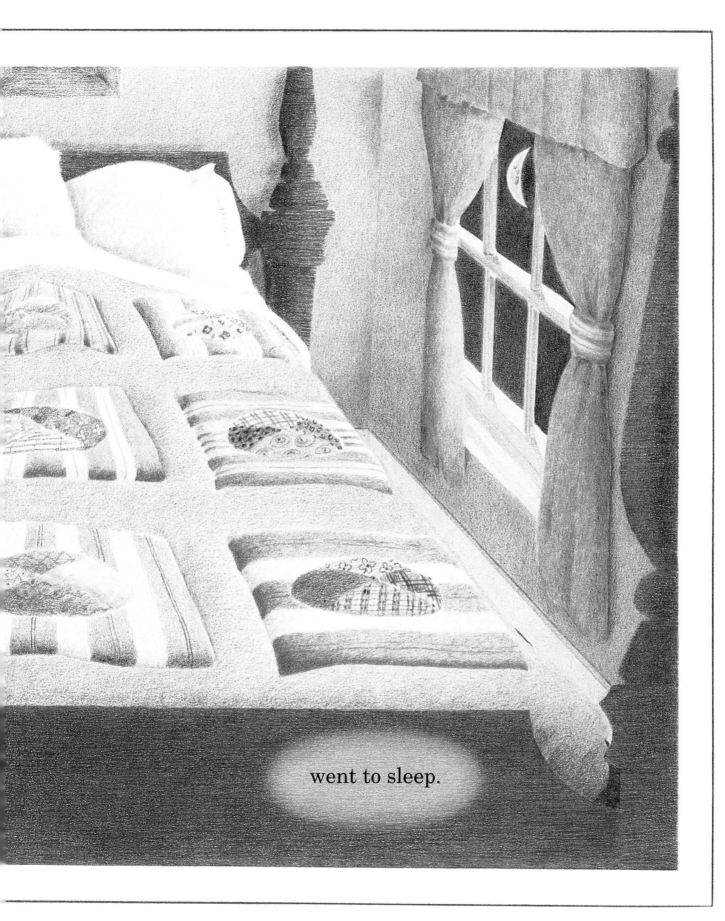

went to sleep.